For my mom and dad
Thank you for always being there and believing in me! Phil. 4:11.
—K.D.

For Dorsey and Helen
You are an example to me of what it means
to be a good mom and dad. I am blessed to have you in my life.
—J.D.

Pete the Cat and His Magic Sunglasses
Text copyright © 2013 by Kimberly and James Dean
Illustrations copyright © 2013 by James Dean
All rights reserved. Printed and manufactured in Heshan City, China.
No part of this book may be used or reproduced in any manner whatsoever
without written permission except in the case of brief quotations embodied in critical articles
and reviews. For information address HarperCollins Children's Books, a division of HarperCollins Publishers,
195 Broadway, New York, NY 10007.
www.harpercollinschildrens.com
ISBN 978-0-06-264098-7
The artist used pen and ink, with watercolor and acrylic paint, on 300lb hot press paper to create the
illustrations for this book.
Typography by Jeanne L. Hogle
17 18 19 20 21    LEO    10 9 8 7 6 5 4 3 2 1
❖
July 2017

# Pete the Cat

## and His Magic Sunglasses

Illustrated by
**James Dean**

Story by
**Kimberly and
James Dean**

HARPER
An Imprint of HarperCollins*Publishers*

Pete the Cat did not feel happy. Pete had never, ever, ever, ever been grumpy before. Pete had the blue cat blues.

Then, as if things were not bad enough, along came Grumpy Toad. Grumpy Toad was never happy! He always wore a frown.

But Grumpy Toad was not GRUMPY today.
He said, "These COOL, BLUE, MAGIC sunglasses
make the blues go away.

They help you see things in a whole new way."

Pete put on the COOL, BLUE, MAGIC sunglasses.
He looked all around.

"RIGHT ON!

The birds are singing.
The sky is bright.
The sun is shining.
I'm feeling ALRIGHT!"

Pete thanked Grumpy Toad for the COOL, BLUE, MAGIC sunglasses. He went on his way, and soon he saw Squirrel. Squirrel did not look happy. Pete said,

"What's wrong, Squirrel?"

Pete said, "Try these COOL, BLUE, MAGIC sunglasses. They help you see things in a whole new way."

Squirrel put on the COOL, BLUE, MAGIC sunglasses and looked all around.

"AWESOME!

The birds are singing.
The sky is bright.
The sun is shining.
I'm feeling ALRIGHT!"

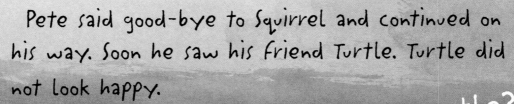

Pete said good-bye to Squirrel and continued on his way. Soon he saw his friend Turtle. Turtle did not look happy.

"What's wrong, Turtle?" Pete asked.

# "I'M SO FRUSTRATED!

Nothing is going my way. I am all upside down today."

Pete said, "Try these COOL, BLUE, MAGIC sunglasses. They help you see things in a whole new way."

Turtle put on the COOL, BLUE, MAGIC
sunglasses and looked all around.

"FAR OUT!

The birds are singing.
The sky is bright.

The sun is shining.
I'm feeling ALRIGHT!"

Pete kept rolling along until he saw Alligator.
Alligator did not look happy.

"What's wrong, Alligator?"
Pete asked.

"I'M SO SAD!

Nothing is going my way. No one wants to play with me today."

Pete said, "Try these COOL, BLUE, MAGIC sunglasses. They help you see things in a whole new way."

Alligator put on the COOL, BLUE, MAGIC sunglasses and looked all around.

"ROCKIN'!

Pete was rolling along and feeling ALRIGHT
when suddenly he fell back.

The COOL, BLUE, MAGIC sunglasses went CRACK.
Uh-oh! Pete didn't know what to do without
those sunglasses.

Just then, Pete looked up at the tree.
Wise Old Owl said, "Pete, you don't need
magic sunglasses to see things in a new way.
Just remember to look for the good in
every day."

Pete looked around without his sunglasses.

"TOO COOL!

The birds are singing.

The sky is bright.

The sun is shining.